HOW PEOPLE LIVE

IN THE MOUNTAINS

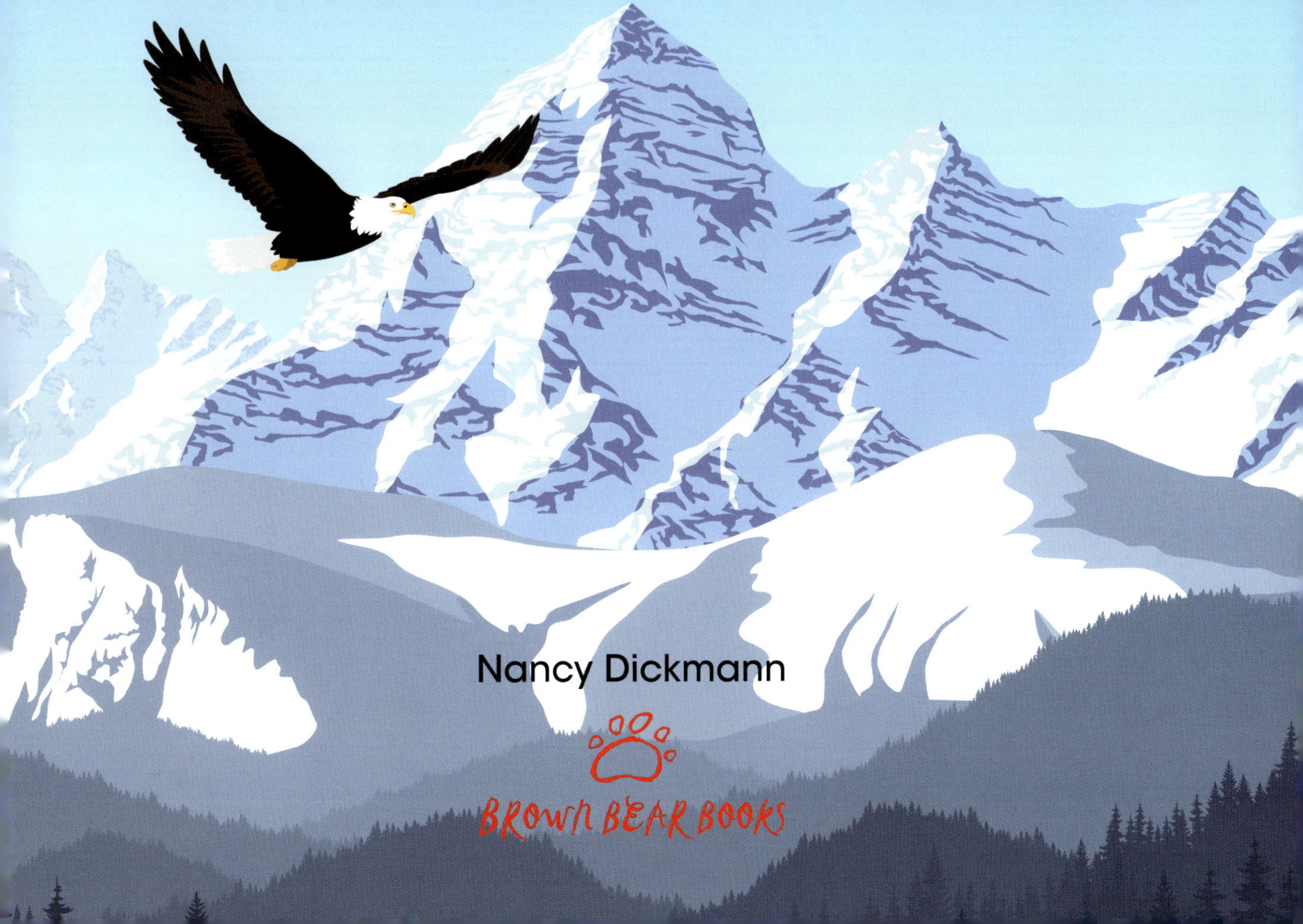

Nancy Dickmann

BROWN BEAR BOOKS

Published by Brown Bear Books Ltd
4877 N. Circulo Bujia, Tucson, AZ 85718, USA
and
Studio G14, Regent Studios, 1 Thane Villas, London N7 7PH, UK

Text: Nancy Dickmann
Design Manager: Keith Davis
Children's Publisher: Anne O'Daly

Library of Congress Cataloging-in-Publication Data
Names: Dickmann, Nancy, author.
Title: In the mountains / Nancy Dickmann.
Description: Tuscon, AZ : Brown Bear Books Ltd., [2025] | Series: Fast Track: How People Live | Includes bibliographical references and index. | Audience: Ages 5-7 years | Audience: Grades K-1 | Summary: "How people live in mountains all around the world"– Provided by publisher.
Identifiers: LCCN 2023052207 (print) | LCCN 2023052208 (ebook) | ISBN 9781781219737 (library binding) | ISBN 9781781219799 (paperback) | ISBN 9781781219850 (ebook)
Subjects: LCSH: Mountain life–Juvenile literature. | Mountain people–Dwellings–Juvenile literature. | Mountains–Recreational use–Juvenile literature.
Classification: LCC GF57 .D53 2025 (print) | LCC GF57 (ebook) | DDC 307.720914/3–dc23/eng/20231221
LC record available at https://lccn.loc.gov/2023052207
LC ebook record available at https://lccn.loc.gov/2023052208

The photographs in this book are used by permission and through the courtesy of:
Cover: Shutterstock BGStock72. Interior: iStock: Serban Bogdan 21-22c, Steve Graham 8-9bk, 16-17bk, Kbels 10-11bk, 18-19 bk, MuchMania 6-7bl, 14-15bk, oliveromg 16; Shutterstock: ActiveLines 4-5bk, 12-13bk, Asmakhan992 5, B. Miriam 10, Danica Chang 12, Osaze Cuomo 8, Keshav Dulal 13, Anna Efimova 9, Omri Eliyahu 21cr, Gorilla Images 21t, HeyPhoto 17, Elena Istomina 3inset, Angelito de Jesus 19, Roman Lysogor 6, Kiego Vargas Nasser 23b, Kenz Nyuyen 11, Sergey Novikov 15, Sergey Onyshko 7, Daria Riabets 1inset, 24br, Evgenii Salienko 18, SaveJungle 1, 2-3, 20-21bk, 22-23bk, 24, TLF Images 21b, Vixit 4, Wayfarerlife 20b, Margaret Wiktor 20t, Zzvet 14.
t-top, b-bottom, l-left, r-right, c-center, bk-background
All other artwork and photography © Brown Bear Books.

Brown Bear Books has made every attempt to contact the copyright holders. If you have any information about omissions please contact: licensing@brownbearbooks.co.uk.

The website addresses in this book were valid at the time of going to press. However, it is possible that contents or addresses may change following publication of this book. No responsibility for any such changes can be accepted by the author or the publisher. Readers should be supervised when they access the Internet.

Words in **bold** appear in the Words to Know on page 23.

Manufactured in the United States of America
CPSIA compliance information: Batch#AG/5659

Contents

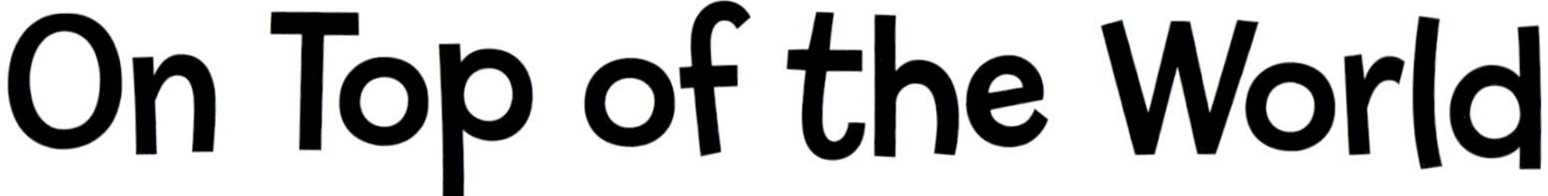

On Top of the World

Mountains are the highest places on Earth.
They are much higher than the tallest buildings.
Some people like to hike on mountains.
Others climb to the top. They look at the view.

Mount Everest is the world's highest mountain. It sticks up above the clouds.

Some animals live high in the mountains. They are **adapted** to the conditions there. People live in mountains, too. Their lives are different from people who live lower down.

WOW!

Snow leopards have wide paws. The paws act like snowshoes. The leopard doesn't sink into the snow.

Weather and Climate

The higher you go, the colder it gets.

High mountains are often very cold.

Some are covered in snow all year round.

It can be very windy.

Sometimes a lot of snow falls down a mountain. This is called an avalanche.

The air is thin high in the mountains. There is less **oxygen**. Some people are used to living here. Their bodies are good at using oxygen. They can get by with less.

Mountain Homes

Mountains don't have much flat land.
Houses are often built onto a slope.
Heavy snow could crush a building.
Mountain homes must be strong.

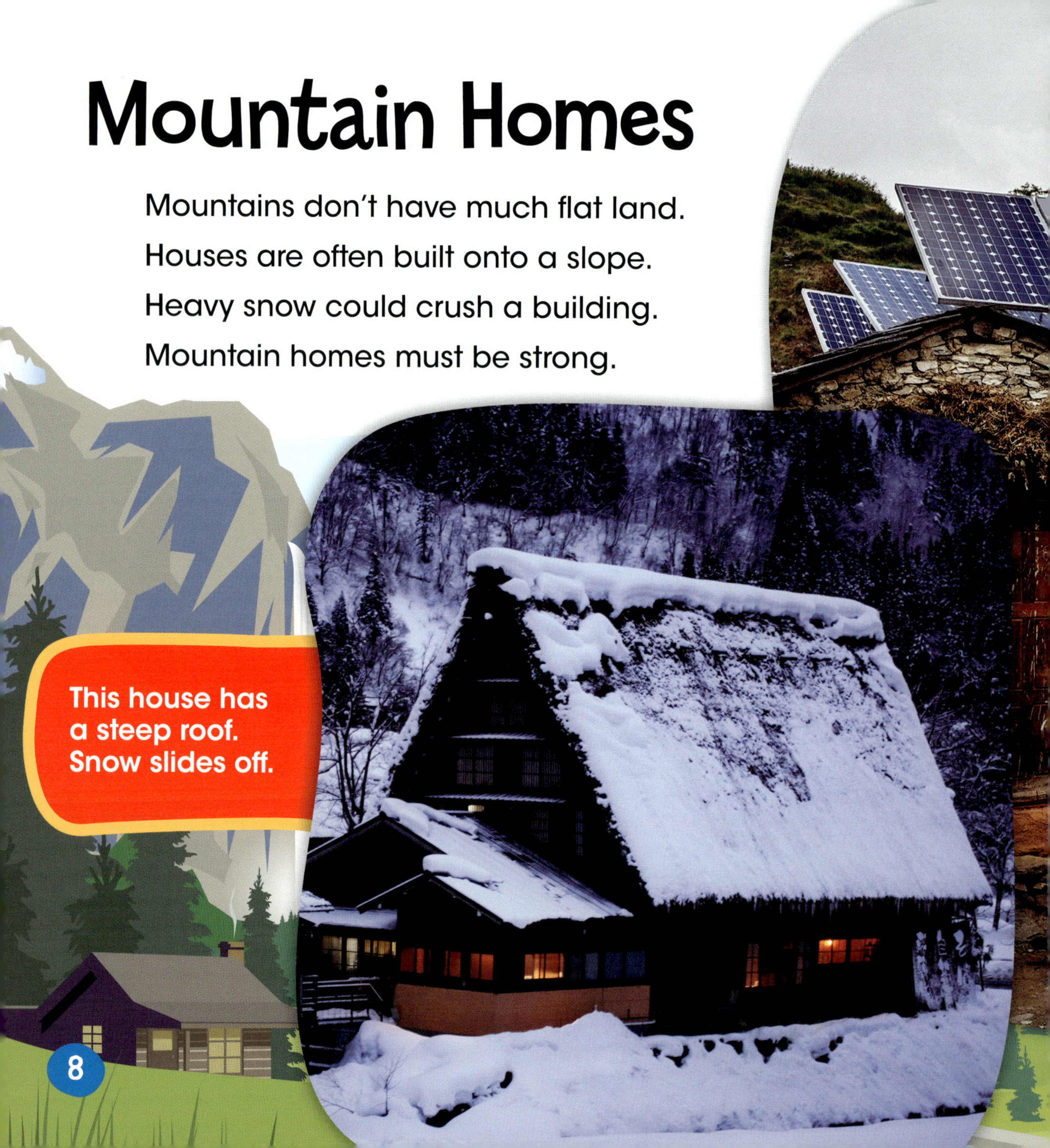

This house has a steep roof. Snow slides off.

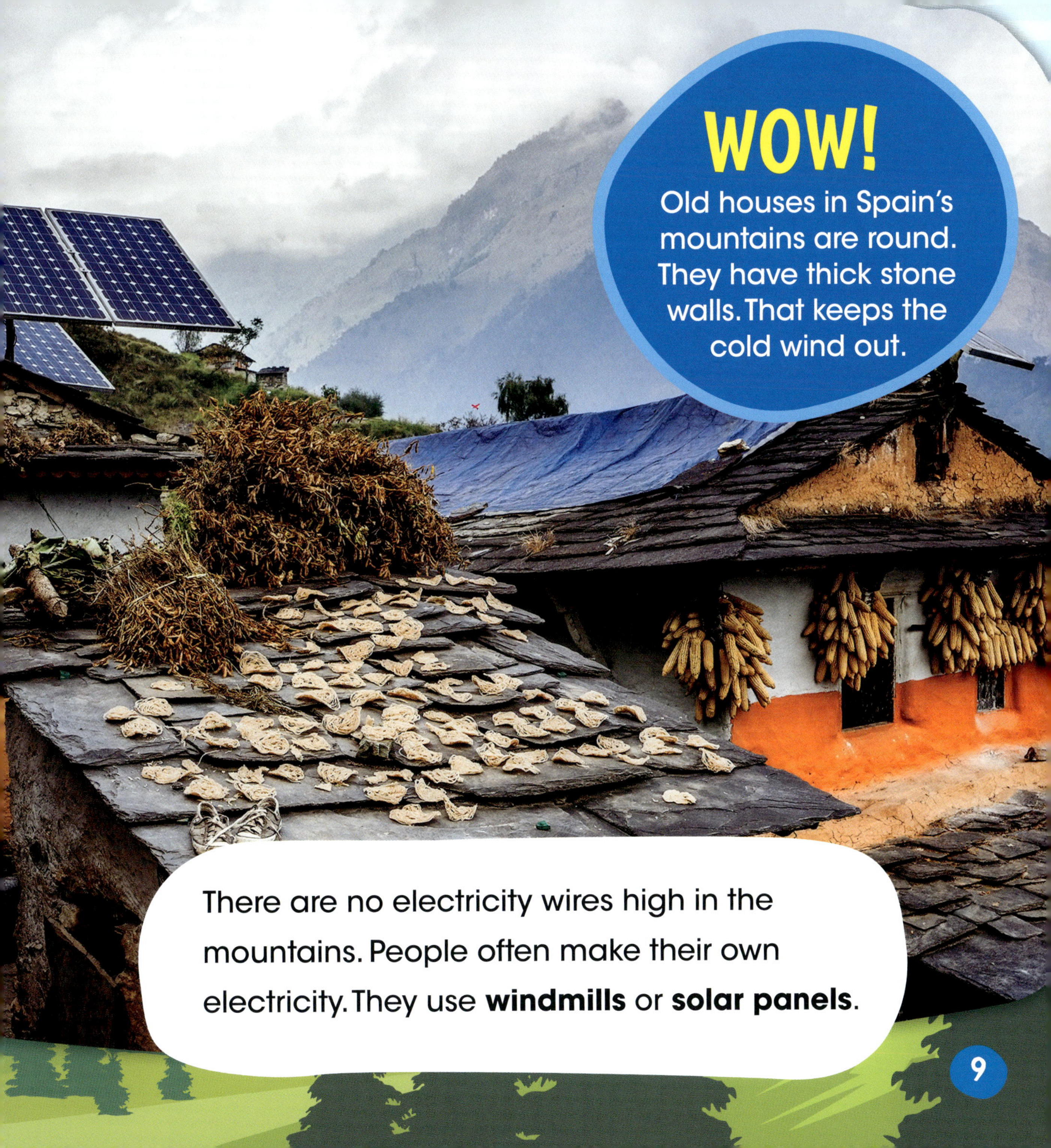

WOW!

Old houses in Spain's mountains are round. They have thick stone walls. That keeps the cold wind out.

There are no electricity wires high in the mountains. People often make their own electricity. They use **windmills** or **solar panels**.

Food and Drink

Some mountains have roads and railroads. Trucks and trains bring food to people there. Other mountain areas are harder to reach. People grow their own food.

The Andes Mountains are in South America. Potatoes grow well here.

Most fields are flat. But mountains are steep. Farmers cut **terraces** into the slopes. The terraces are like steps. The steps are flat. That's where **crops** grow.

Clothes

Mountains can be cold and windy.
People need warm clothes.
In the Andes, people raise llamas.
They use their wool to make clothes.

Llamas have thick coats. The wool is used for blankets and clothes.

In the Himalayas, people raise yaks.
Yaks have long, shaggy fur.
People spin it to make **yarn**.
They turn the yarn into cloth.

WOW!

A yak's coat has different layers. The outer layer is very tough. People use it to make ropes and tents.

Jobs

Many mountain people live simply. They grow crops. They raise animals. They build homes and weave cloth. Some make crafts to sell to **tourists**.

Tourists visit mountain areas. Local people work as guides. It's a good way to earn money.

WOW!

People build big **telescopes** on mountains. Scientists work there. They look at stars and planets.

Some people visit mountains to ski. This makes jobs for local people. Some teach visitors how to ski. Others work in hotels or restaurants.

Getting Around

Getting around can be hard work.

The ground is steep. It is hard to build roads.

Many roads run along **valleys**. It is flatter there.

Snow and ice make driving dangerous. People use chains on tires. It gives the tires more grip.

WOW!

Mountain trains can climb steep slopes. They have special wheels that "crawl" along the tracks.

Some people use skis to get around.
Other people travel on sleds.
Snowmobiles are like skis with an engine!
They move fast across snow.

Games and Sports

Many people climb mountains.

But mountain climbing can be dangerous.

High up, the air is thin. There is not enough oxygen.

Climbers carry tanks of oxygen.

Mountain climbers use ropes. They wear special boots. A helmet protects their head.

Mountains are great to visit.
In the summer, people come to hike.
In winter, they zoom downhill
on skis and snowboards!

Where in the World?

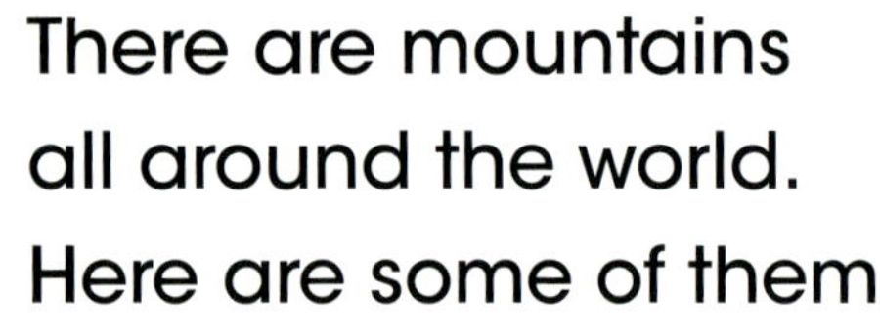

There are mountains all around the world. Here are some of them.

The Rocky Mountains are in the western United States.

The Andes run down the west coast of South America.

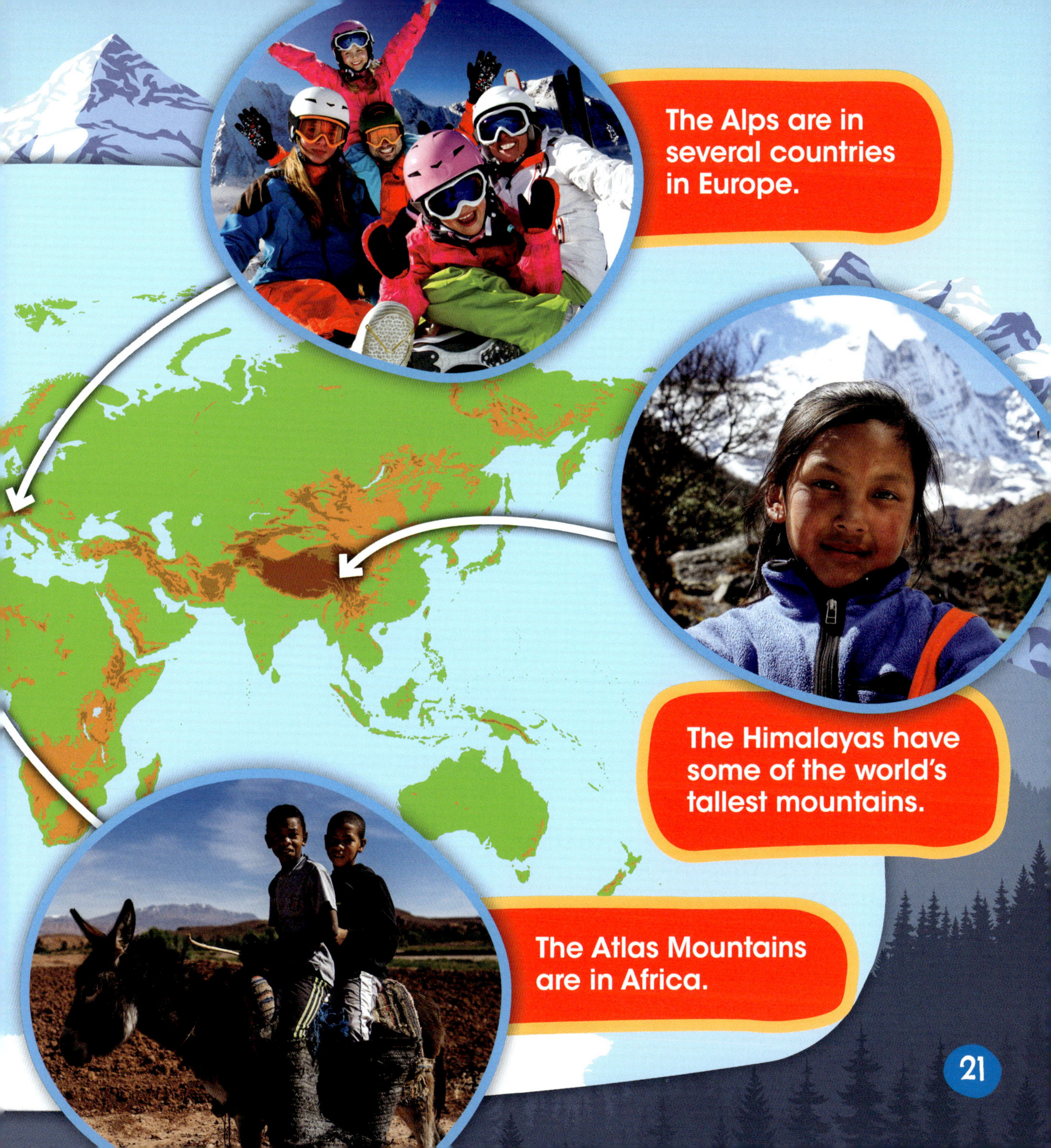
The Alps are in several countries in Europe.
The Himalayas have some of the world's tallest mountains.
The Atlas Mountains are in Africa.

Activities

Look on a map and find the mountains that are closest to where you live. How far away are they? Use the map scale to figure it out.

Design your dream mountain house. What would it look like? How would it keep you warm and safe?

Did you know that some of Earth's mountains are under the sea? These "seamounts" are home to many sea creatures. Research some of the animals that live on seamounts.

Find Out More

Websites

ducksters.com/geography/mountain_ranges.php

kids.britannica.com/kids/article/mountain/346179

kids.nationalgeographic.com/nature/habitats/article/mountain

Books

Mountains Lisa J. Amstutz, Capstone 2021

Mountains: Explore Earth's Majestic Mountain Habitats Charlotte Guillain, words & pictures 2020

Top of the World: Off-Grid Mountain Living Mari Bolte, Lerner Books 2023

Words to Know

adapted having a change in body or behavior that helps a plant or animal survive in its habitat

avalanche a large amount of snow that tumbles down the side of a mountain

crops plants that people grow to eat

oxygen a gas in the air which humans need to breathe

solar panel a flat panel that can turn sunlight into electricity

telescope a tool for seeing things far away

terraces strips of flat land cut into the side of a mountain

tourist a person who travels to a place on vacation

valley an area of lower land between hills or mountains, often with a river flowing through it

windmill a structure that uses the wind's energy to make electricity, grind grain, or pump water

yarn thread that is used to make cloth

Index